A Note to Parents

For many children, learning math is difficult and "I hate math!" is their first response — to which many parents silently add "Me, too!" Children often see adults comfortably reading and writing, but they rarely have such models for mathematics. And math fear can be catching!

The easy-to-read stories in this *Hello Math* series were written to give children a positive introduction to mathematics, and parents a pleasurable re-acquaintance with a subject that is important to everyone's life. *Hello Math* stories make mathematical ideas accessible, interesting, and fun for children. The activities and suggestions at the end of each book provide parents with a hands-on approach to help children develop mathematical interest and confidence.

Enjoy the mathematics!

• Give your child a chance to retell the story. The more familiar children are with the story, the more they will understand its mathematical concepts.

• Use the colorful illustrations to help children "hear and see" the math at work in the story.

• Treat the math activities as games to be played for fun. Follow your child's lead. Spend time on those activities that engage your child's interest and curiosity.

• Activities, especially ones using physical materials, help make abstract mathematical ideas concrete.

Learning is a messy process. Learning about math calls for children to become immersed in lively experiences that help them make sense of mathematical concepts and symbols.

Although learning about numbers is basic to math, other ideas, such as identifying shapes and patterns, measuring, collecting and interpreting data, reasoning logically, and thinking about chance, are also important. By reading these stories and having fun with the activities, you will help your child enthusiastically say *"Hello, Math,"* instead of "I hate math."

—Marilyn Burns
National Mathematics Educator
Author of *The I Hate Mathematics! Book*

For Nancy Smiler Levinson
—J.R.

ISBN 0-590-67359-9

Copyright © 1996 by Scholastic Inc.
The activities on pages 43-48 copyright © 1996 by Marilyn Burns.
All rights reserved. Published by Scholastic Inc.
CARTWHEEL BOOKS and the CARTWHEEL BOOKS logo
are registered trademarks of Scholastic Inc.
HELLO MATH READER and the HELLO MATH READER logo
are trademarks of Scholastic Inc.

Library of Congress Cataloging-in-Publication Data

Rocklin, Joanne.
    The case of the missing birthday party / by Joanne Rocklin; illustrated by
John Speirs; math activities by Marilyn Burns.
        p.   cm. — (Hello math reader. Level 4)
    Summary: Liz the Whiz & Co. help a neighbor find her way to a birthday
party by using their knowledge of place value.
    ISBN 0-590-67359-9
    [1. Mathematics — Fiction. 2. Birthdays — Fiction.]
    I. Speirs, John, ill. II. Burns, Marilyn. III. Title. IV. Series.
PZ7.R59Cas 1997
[Fic]—dc20   96-14841
                                                             CIP
                                                             AC

12 11 10 9 8 7 6 5 4 3 2 1   6 7 8 9/9 0 1/0

Printed in the U.S.A.   23

First Scholastic printing, November 1996

THE CASE OF
THE MISSING
BIRTHDAY PARTY

by Joanne Rocklin
Illustrated by John Speirs
Math Activities by Marilyn Burns

Hello Math Reader — Level 4

SCHOLASTIC INC.
Cartwheel BOOKS®
New York Toronto London Auckland Sydney

My name is Liz.
Here is my card:

Henry is my little brother.
He's a Whiz-in-Training (WIT).

GOT A PROBLEM?
LIZ THE WHIZ & CO.
WILL SOLVE IT.

Marv is our dog.
He's smarter than he looks.
Marv's Nose Always Knows.

Henry, Marv, and I are a great team.

It's Saturday.
Henry and I are sitting on the front steps.
Marv is sleeping.
I say, "Nothing is going on around here."
Marv snores.
"Another boring Saturday," I say.
"Right," says Henry, the WIT.

Boy, are we wrong!

I jump up from the steps.
"What's that sound?" I ask.
Henry listens.
I listen.
Marv listens.
Somebody is crying!
It is our neighbor Pauline,
coming down our block.
There are ten houses
on each block.
Remember that fact.

"What's wrong?" I ask Pauline.
"Waa-hh!!" answers Pauline.
I look at Pauline's dress.
It is a pink dress with lots of bows.
I look at the box she is carrying.
More bows. Wrapping paper.
I, Liz the Whiz, put all the clues together.
"Where's the party?" I ask.
Pauline isn't talking.
"WAA-HH!" she cries.
"Get her a drink," I say to Henry.

Pauline is sipping her lemonade.
Marv is sniffing at the present.
I, Liz the Whiz, take a closer look.
Why is the bow on the present
all chewed up?
I decide to remember that fact.

PARTI
5
TWIG STR

SAT 12PM

Pauline tells her story:
"I was invited to Nick's
birthday party around the corner
at 5 Twig Street.
I rang the doorbell there but—"
Pauline takes another sip
of her lemonade.
"Go on," says Henry.
"WAA-HH!!" says Pauline.
Pauline isn't talking anymore.
"Let's check out 5 Twig,"
I say to my partner.
"Right," says Henry, the WIT.

We ring the doorbell at 5 Twig Street.
Nobody answers.
We ring again.
At last a woman opens the door.
She has yellow paint on her nose.
She is wearing old clothes.
She is holding a paintbrush.

I, Liz the Whiz, put all
the clues together.
"I guess there's no party at
your house," I say.
The woman laughs. "That's
what I told your friend."

"Are you sure you have the right address,
Pauline?" asks Henry, the WIT.
Pauline holds up the party invitation.
It is full of holes!

Suddenly, I, Liz the Whiz, put the clues together once again.
"Pauline, do you have a new pet?" I ask.

"Yes, I do," Pauline says.
"My sweet hamster Spotty."
I grab the invitation. "Look!" I shout.
"Your sweet hamster Spotty
chewed holes all over this invitation!
The party is not at 5 Twig Street.
I'll bet Nick's address has two digits.

"I'll bet the five is really in the ones' place.
And the tens' place is all chewed up!"

"You mean — ?" asks Henry, the WIT.
"Yes! The party is at something-5
Twig Street. Let's go!" I say.

We knock at 15 Twig Street.
We knock at 25 Twig Street.
We knock at 35 Twig and
ring the doorbell at 45.

No party.
No party.
No answer.
No party.

"WAA-HH!" cries Pauline. "We'll never find it."
"Wait!" I, Liz the Whiz, say.
"I'm going home to play with my sweet hamster
Spotty," says Pauline.
"I just thought of something else!" I say.
"We're headed for 55 Twig. But suppose the 5 is in
the tens' place. Then what, WIT?"

Henry thinks hard. "Then the party could be at —"
"Right! Any of the 50-somethings on Twig Street!"

We rush to the next block. Henry and Pauline try
the houses with even-numbered addresses.
Marv and I try the houses with
odd-numbered addresses.
Nothing.

This last house is empty.
There is a FOR SALE sign in front.
Marv goes to sleep on the grass.
We sit down beside Marv.
We need a rest.
I look at the invitation again.
Pretty chewed up.
Then I, Liz the Whiz, have a terrible
thought.

"Oh, no!" I say.
"Suppose the five is in the hundreds' place
instead of the tens' place.
Suppose the tens' and the ones' places
were *both* chewed up!"

"You mean—?" asks Henry, the WIT.

"Yes," I say. "Maybe Nick's address
is a *three*-digit number!
Maybe the party is at
500-something Twig Street!"
"But look —" says the WIT.
He points to my map on the sidewalk.
"There are ten houses on each block . . ."
Henry says.

"... and Twig Street is ten blocks
long," I add.
"That's only 100 houses,"
says the WIT.
"Good thinking!" I say. "There *are no*
500-something houses on Twig Street."
"WAA-HH!" Pauline wails.
"Now WHAA-TT?"

I look at Henry. "Well, WIT, we won't find the party at 500-something Twig Street," I say.
"Nick's probably blowing out the birthday candles right now!" Pauline says.
Henry looks at me. "Or 50-something Twig Street," he says.

Pauline sobs. "Soon the birthday cake will be all gone!"

"We already checked 5, 15, and 25 Twig," I say.

"And 35 and 45," the WIT adds.

"Wait a minute!" I say.
All those 5s.
We were looking in the right place all along.
I, Liz the Whiz, look at Henry
and Henry looks at me.
We are both thinking the same thing —
we must keep going *up* Twig Street.
"WAA-HH!" Pauline cries.
"RUFF-RUFF!" Marv barks.

I look up Twig Street.
Marv is barking and jumping now.
I take a longer look. Then I see her.
She's wearing a red dress.
She's carrying something.
And she's in a big hurry.
"After her!" I cry.

I grab Marv's leash.
Henry grabs Pauline's hand.
We follow the girl.

We race past 65 Twig and start to catch up
with her.
I can see she's wearing a fancy dress.
Remember that fact.

We race past 75 Twig and close in on her.
She's got a box with something written on it
under her arm.
Remember that fact, too.

The girl turns up a walkway.
We're right behind her.
I get a look at the mailbox.
85.
I get a look at what's on the girl's box.
Happy Birthday. Happy Birthday.
Happy Birthday.

Marv runs up and sniffs. He barks.
The Nose Always Knows a birthday
cake when he smells one.

I put two and two together.
"We're here," I cry.

"Thank you!" says Pauline.
"You're a whiz!" says the WIT.
"Case closed," I say.

• ABOUT THE ACTIVITIES •

Children compare numbers by relying on their ability to count. They know that 85 is larger than 58 because "85 comes after 58." However, not many young children notice or can explain the significance of where digits are placed in numbers. The story and activities in this book help children see the usefulness of knowing about place value.

Our place value system, which makes it possible for us to represent any number with the ten digits from 0 through 9, is not simple. Children must learn that the value of each digit in a number depends on its position. These activities provide ways for children to think about the tens and ones structure of our number system. And all the directions are written for you to read along with your child.

As with all complex ideas, learning requires time. Don't worry if some of the activities are too difficult for your child or if your child isn't interested. With time, all children figure out how tens and ones work. Be open to your child's interests, and have fun with math!

— Marilyn Burns

You'll find tips and suggestions
for guiding the activities whenever
you see a box like this!

Retelling the Story

Early in the story, Liz the Whiz decided to remember two facts:

There are ten houses on each block.

The bow on the birthday present was all chewed up.

How did each of these clues help Liz solve the mystery?

What other clues did she use?

Children may have different ideas about the usefulness of these clues. If you don't think your child's reasoning makes sense, rather than correcting him or her, offer your idea for consideration.

Liz, Henry, Pauline, and Marv found out that the party was not at 5 Twig Street. Liz decided to check all the houses that had a 5 at the end of their address — 15, 25, 35, and 45 Twig Street. What other numbers can you think of that end with a 5?

When they were heading for 55 Twig Street, Liz thought of something else. The "5" on the invitation could be in the tens place, so the party might be at *any* of the 50-something houses on Twig Street. How many 50-something houses are there? How many are even numbers and how many are odd?

If your child isn't sure about how many numbers there are in the 50s, it may help to write out the numbers. Also, if your child doesn't know which numbers are odd and which are even, you may be interested in reading *Even Steven and Odd Todd*, a Hello Math Reader that helps children learn about even and odd numbers.

Liz then thought that the house number could have three digits, with a 5 in the hundreds place. That would mean the party was at 500-something Twig Street. But Henry and Liz figured out that 500-something Twig Street wasn't possible. How did the clue that Twig Street was only ten blocks long help Henry and Liz figure this out?

It's a good thing that there weren't any 500-something houses on Twig Street. That would be a lot of houses to check! How many numbers are there in the five hundreds? Can you write all of them? How long do you think it would take you?

After ruling out 5, 15, 25, 35, 45, and all of the 50-something houses on Twig Street, several other clues finally helped Liz and the others find the birthday party. What were they? How did each of these clues help solve the mystery?

What's My Number?

This is a guessing game for you to play with another person.

Think of a number from 1 to 100 and give a clue: My number has a __ in the tens' place.

"My number has a four in the tens' place.

? 4 ?

Have your partner try to guess your number.

Keep track of how many guesses he or she takes to get your number.

Play again so you have a chance to guess.

Now try the game another way. This time give a clue like this: My number has a __ in the ones' place.

If you are guessing, would you rather have a clue about the number in the tens' place or the number in the ones' place? Why?

The Place Value Game

This is a game for two or more people. The goal is to make the highest three-digit number possible.

Each player needs a sheet of paper and a pencil. Also, cut up ten small slips of paper, number them from 0 to 9, and put them in a bag. Then, each of you should draw four boxes on your paper like the ones shown here. Make the boxes large enough so you can write a number in each.

To play, follow the rules on the next page.

The Place Value Game Rules

1. One player reaches into the bag (without looking) and removes a slip of paper. Let everyone see the number on it.

2. All players write the number on their papers. You can put it in one of the boxes to make a three-digit number. Or you can throw the number away by putting it in the extra box. Once you write a number, you can't move it to another box.

3. Put the number slip back in the bag. Now another player draws a slip. No peeking!

4. Repeat steps 2 and 3 until each player has written four numbers and has filled all four of his or her boxes. The winner is the player with the highest three-digit number.

You can change the rules so that the player with the lowest number wins. Or draw an extra box and play to make four-digit numbers.